The Truth Seeker

Lee Chondo

Miraesung

Meditation

Lee Chondo :

Poet, novelist, and literary critic, Lee Chondo is an active member of various Korean literary associations. He has won several awards including the Korean Literary Criticism Award, the Korean Literature and Art Award and the Midang Literary Award. The Truth Seeker (2014), a long narrative poem, and Love Song of the East (2016) are among his published works.

Translated by Kevin O'Rourke :

Kevin O'Rourke is professor emeritus of English literature at Kyunghee University. He has translated many classical and contemporary Korean literary texts, ranging through hyangga, Koryo kayo, shijo, kasa, hanshi, modern short stories and novellas, notably Yi Munyol's Our Twisted Hero (Hyperion 2001). He has won literary awards in Korea, US and Ireland.

You will not be lonely

because I am in your breath.

I will not be lonely

because you are in my breath.

We will not be lonely

because two measures of loneliness meet in us
and we are now a single breath.

Prologue

The truth seeker is old and sick and faces imminent death. He closes his eyes, drifts into meditation and enters the maze of eternity. His journey begins at night with symptoms of the breakdown of consciousness. Dark unsettling images threaten to suffocate him until he finds himself back in childhood, in his mother's house. Darkness changes to light, the intimate light of the mother-son relationship. As the sense of intimacy between mother and son becomes difficult to maintain, hoof beats ring out in the distance. A messenger from the other world, mal—horse, mal—word comes to guide him. The old man mounts the word-horse and begins a journey through labyrinths of language and symbol, seeking to answer the question, Who am I. The union of horse and rider replicates the intimacy of mother and child, of speaker and spoken word. The quest leads through the recesses of memory to time past. There is darkness and tears, light and exhilaration. The quest ranges through fertile land and desert. The language is difficult, abstract, abstruse, and deeply symbolical, reflecting the complexity of the experience. Even when flooded with light, the old man is never far from tears. Experience is his first poem, his last poem, his every poem. The goal is cosmic enlightenment. Life is one, religion is one, philosophy is one, art is one, horse and rider are one. The old man relives life's loves, losses, desires, sensations, feelings, the real, the unreal, the illusory, creativity, philosophy, religion, myth, everything that makes him who he is. He moves through spheres of action and inaction in an imaginative world of nymphs, centaur, minotaur and sphinx. He meets Aphrodite, Artemis, Diana, Gaea, Don Quixote, Goliath, Diogenes, the Dragon King and his court, the Buddha, Mohammed and the suffering Christ. The quest leads through the 108 defilements, the 108 beads of the Buddhist rosary, the 7 rituals that begin on the day of death and end on the 49th day, and the Christian Way of the Cross. Cosmic unity with God, nature, the universe and man is the focus of the narrative. The desert is everywhere: it is the replete emptiness that fills all things. At the same time it is language, symbol, the unknown world, the world of death, the eternal, and the subconscious. Memories crowd consciousness. The reader is invited to accompany the old man on his journey through memory, to run with him the gamut of human life from Neanderthal man to homo sapiens, and to experience with him the burdens of modern technology. He gets off the horse for the last time. When his feet touch the earth, he becomes a child again and is reunited with his mother. Unity of being is achieved. Mother and son fly off together—two in one—to become a star in the sky. The star is the light of knowledge. The horse, custodian of language and symbol, emblem of unity of being, remains behind.

1

I stood in the depths of the night. I had lost my way. I lifted night's veil and looked everywhere. An elusive loneliness enfolded me. I was caught in the silence of distant uncertainties. I burst into tears, idle tears. Sadness filled my heart. My feelings flowed in mist, rain and tears.

2

I heard a song, a tune of old time, an ancient memory, vaguely distant. I opened the ears of my spirit and gave myself gently to the melody. Time passed. A name brushed by me, tickling my brain like a soft breath. I called out that name as if taking a breath, (Love, my love, my love.)
A lyrical song hovered in the deep of the night. Memories and pain, abstracted glances, plaintive gestures, feather white echoes of loneliness revolved in the thick smog.

3

The song stopped; the melody ceased. Time
passed, too long to calculate. I walked toward the
source of the song. Darkness draped me like a
blanket. I had a sense of suffocating. I wanted to
throw off the blanket of darkness, but the
darkness grew thicker. It wrapped me round.
I lifted my head and looked at the night sky. The
sky had disappeared. No moon, no stars, only the
blackness of empty sky.

4

I was enclosed in fear; an indefinable terror
constricted the uvula at the back of my throat.
I was face to face with my soul, caught in a space
too great to measure. I could barely move my
tongue. (Soul, soul, soul), I called out shakily.
I was trapped in the snare of darkness, a pitiable
skeletal spirit, immersed in the magic of the night.

5

I walked on, insinuating myself into the heart of
the night. I walked into eternity's maze—there
was neither entrance nor exit. I drifted along
time's veins into uncharted space. I stopped and
looked around. I saw a light, a small light, waving
faintly in the distance. I walked toward it. The
light gradually brightened. It was dyed crimson,
then blue. When eventually I reached the light,
I saw that it was the radiance of the unknown,
a large round mass of light, a strange agglomerate
of millions of fireflies. Suddenly the light flew
over my head like silver powder. Then it
disappeared. A great inky darkness ensued, a dull,
gentle, black light. I was a tiny particle within it,
an essence, a formless self-consciousness
hovering on the boundaries of space-time.

6

Light, light, light. I could see light everywhere.
The pores of darkness had gradually reopened:
it was a commendable return. Innumerable stars
were scattered through the night sky: they were
the shining flower-smiles of the dead. I lifted my
head and looked at the star clusters. They poured
into my old veins like the Milky Way of
childhood. Darkness all around me. The earth on
which the star clusters looked down lay in silence,
a primordial quiet whose depths could not be
measured. An inexplicable sadness filled me. It
rode my sensibilities through long time and took
my heart into the distant recesses of memory.

7

I saw the vague outline of something in the dark.
A narrow alleyway. A boy was playing in front of
the gate of a house. His mother called him.
The boy ran to her. An attractive young woman
stood smiling in the front yard. Beautiful,
unsophisticated, she opened her arms. The
washing hung on the clothesline. The boy ran into
his mother's arms. She hugged him and kissed his
head. She took him into the house. A small
serving table was arranged in the middle of the
room. A serving cloth with lovely designs lay on
top. She lifted the cloth. The food was simple but
pleasing to the eye. She placed a piece of boned
fish on top of the boy's rice bowl. The boy ate
quickly but with relish. She watched him in
silence, smiling gracefully. It was a scene to
remember, happiness personified, purest joy,
the most uniquely beautiful, opulent prospect you
could ever hope for.

8

I walked across to gate and house, to yard and
clothesline, to mother and son. But the closer I got
the further the scene removed itself from me.
When I took a step forward, the scene moved two
steps away. Then suddenly it was gone, beyond
the darkness. I stood there vacantly, looking at a
formless shadow. I was gripped by an emptiness
that was difficult to bear. I was a lost child, an
animal pelt left alone on the earth. I called my
mother like boys do. (Mother, mother, mother),
I cried. Then I heard the sound of a horse's hooves.
The sound came closer and closer.

9

I got on the horse, grabbed the reins and set off
into the dark. Clip, clip, the mystery of the horse's
hooves echoed in the night air. The sound
reverberated in my heart. It was as if my mother
were patting me gently. I felt the peace a child
knows in the cradle. A feeling of being totally
replete wrapped me round. Joy reigned. I had a
sense of warm comfort. The living, breathing
horse that I was riding, and the echoes the horse
made in the night comforted me body and soul.
For the first time I knew I was not alone.

10

We traveled for a long time in the dark, eventually reaching a river bank. The horse stopped. (Crescent moon) I listened to the river breathing. Moonlight shone on the water, a deep metallic pigment sharp as the blue glint of a honed blade. The horse stood there, immobile, head bowed, as if troubled, looking down at the river bed. Time passed. Suddenly the horse lifted its hooves. Without faltering it walked on the water (as if it were walking on firm ground). Anxiety and fear were forgotten; calm and wonder filled my heart. The horse and I were one.

11

We crossed the river and continued slowly
through uncharted fields. The horse moved gently
as if deep in thought. We walked toward the
horizon of mystery, which lay propped on
starlight at the distant end of the dark. In the black
solitude that covered us, the night breeze tickled
our ears. Wildflower essence, wet with night dew,
wafted under our noses. I grew solemn in the
breath-stopping aura of the sacred that filled the
night with fragrance and in the energy-at-rest
feeling that is in living things. God's holy
providence caressed my body, creating a sense of
the mystery that breathes over us. I felt the
creative and destructive urges that govern things.
I felt these forces within me. Death is not terror
but joy, the forces said. Death and annihilation are
unbounded blessings, they whispered, sublime
ecstasy, perfect grace.

12

The horse came to a small cabin. I got off, gently pushed open the brushwood gate and went into the yard. I stood (in faint moonlight) in the yard and looked around. A single paneled door opened. Sparrows chattered under the eaves. A young girl came out. She wore a ribbon in her hair. She went into the kitchen and returned with a gourd dipper. She came over to me and handed me the dipper. I took a few mouthfuls. The water tasted cold and sweet. My languid body cells woke up; the water filled me body and spirit. I went to give back the dipper, but the girl had disappeared. I put the dipper on the verandah and left the yard.

13

I mounted the horse and moved slowly away from the cabin. I didn't look back, but I felt the eyes of the girl looking at me from the cabin door. I sighed deeply. My eyes were wet. Cold turmoil whirled in my heart. Suddenly I was a boy again, filled with memories of running to the cabin, yes, running, running toward that girl. And now all that sits on the horse is a bag of old bones and memories, a withered ghost, a dried-out skin.

14

Star clusters were still scattered through the sky. We continued on through the fields; overhead a sky of jeweled stars, underfoot the silent earth. Suddenly I had a sense of infinite benevolence, holy tolerance. I was nestling in the arms of God. I listened to my inner rhythms. My breathing was like the sound of eternity. It wrapped me snugly like a heavenly blanket. I entrusted myself to God's arms as if in a dream. I slept like a child on the breast, like a baby bird. I savored the taste of oblivescence.

15

The horse stopped. (Full moon) A one-storey,
dilapidated wine house stood in front. I got off the
horse. The door was closed. A boisterous clamor
came from within. I opened the wine house door
and stepped inside. (The customers, surprised by
the sound of the door, stopped talking and turned
to look at me.) It was a fusty smelling place with
rough tables, a sort of cave structure with a
gloomy atmosphere. The customers were all
dressed shabbily like farmers. They looked at me
with suspicion and distrust as if I were an
uninvited guest intruding on a private gathering.
Their eyes were docile but wary, honest but
intense. I was different. I gave off a sense of
inherent rejection, which they felt in my person
and in the clothes I was wearing. My hair was
white, brushed neatly back from the front and
I wore a dapper frock coat.

16

In an attempt to change the atmosphere, I called for an extra bottle of wine at every table--the best in the house, I said. A delighted older woman approached. Plump faced, she wore an apron and she had a scarf around her head. I couldn't say whether she was the madam of the wine house or the woman of the house. She directed me to a seat inside. I sat down on a wooden chair with no back. By now the customers had forgotten me and were back to their old selves. They lifted their bowls with coarse, dark hands and talked among themselves. Perhaps one or two cast unfriendly glances at me, but even these soon looked away. An anchor without an anchor chain hung on one wall. An extra bottle arrived at every table. They poured the wine nonchalantly, filling each other's bowls and downing them in a single gulp.

17

I came out of the wine house and mounted the horse. I felt a little light-headed. The horse lifted its hooves and took a few strides forward. I looked up at the stars. The light of a myriad sparkling stars filled my eyes. Starlight flooded my sight. (Are you aware of man's beauty) I muttered— (not the smile that appears to the eye, but the shadow of sadness within the eye? Are you aware of the beauty of existence—not the strength apparent to the eye, but the weakness that human nature conceals within?) I smiled gently. The sadness draped within me was not revealed. No one could see my turmoil. Deep night prevailed. The darkness was dyed a deeper blue.

18

The horse walked on through the dark, its stride
so gentle and sweet I fell into reverie on its back.
How can I describe the feeling? Something
gracious and noble, not easily put into words:
a sense of sublime beauty encircled me. The horse
and I were no longer two. One and one had met in
two. We had always been one. As life and death
are not two, as bloom and wither are not two, as
come and go are not two, as being and non-being
are not two, so too the horse and I felt that we had
always been one.

19

I was not afraid. I was content, at peace. The horse was God's messenger leading me to nirvana, and I was walking my last moments in this world. Scenes from my youth swept in front of me, closely followed by a favored phrase from the past, (Heart, you must dream a holy revolution). It was a catchword of youth, a conviction, a pristine attachment. All my life I had dreamed a holy revolution. But nothing came of it. I achieved nothing. I reached nowhere. It was a false road, a vain dream, a floating cloud. And now, old and sick, having never realized my dream, I am approaching death. I confess readily: I have no regrets, no sadness, no feeling of failure. I dreamed a dream. I lived the dream, and I am dying with the dream.

20

I looked at the night sky. Flickering starlight
smiles filtered into my eyes. I reached a hand
toward the stars. A fallen star dropped into my
palm. It was like a mysterious flower, glowing
like a fairy in a children's story. A little later,
I tossed the star back into the night sky. It hovered
on the edge of the sky, blinked its starry eye and
looked down at me. A voice from an unknown
world brushed past me. Who was it? I heard a
whisper in my ear. (You'll be a star, a star, a star.)

21

The horse pulled up. A desert stretched like
eternity into the distance—the world of the
unknown. Stars, darkness and sand formed a stage
for illusion to play on. We stood for a long time
on that stage. Suddenly I burst into tears. Not
from sadness or regret or longing, but from the
awareness of a magnificent hand, from the
wonder of God's presence, from awe in the face
of the absolute, from a fundamental respect and
reverence. The aesthetic enchantment, the sheer
shock of everything around me was too much to
bear. I got off the horse and squatted on the
ground. I wrapped my arms around my knees like
a boy and buried my head. And for a long time
I cried silently.

22

I got back up on the horse. We continued on
through the desert. An arid world without a blade
of grass. We crossed the desert, moving inexorably
over the sloping sands. No matter how far we
went, I felt we were marking time in one place,
with no end in sight. I saw a gigantic pyramid
rising in the starlight in front. It got gradually
closer. Then the outline of the pyramid grew
gradually distant, making me aware of moving
through space. Head slanted, I was buried in
thought. One idea occupied my head (I am alone,
like freedom; and being alone, I am free). People
often ask, (Are you not lonely?) I answer with a
smile. (How about you, are you not lonely?)
They do not reply, but I know what they are
feeling. They are lonelier than me and I live
alone. They are at pains to hide their feelings,
but I hear the unvoiced reply. Sad looks and
empty smiles whisper the truth.

23

I put a brake on my thoughts and looked around.
It was the middle of the desert. The horse stood
there, looking down. The moon had disappeared
among the stars (Where was it hiding?) Suddenly
a lamp appeared at a little distance. I got off the
horse. I walked toward the lamp and stopped in
front of it. A strange form stood there. From the
shoulders down it was a man, but the head was
that of a goat. It stood there holding the lamp.
The goat asked, (Traveler, what is the meaning of
life?) (Life is being alive,) I replied. (It's a long
road, but when you live your allotted span, you'll
find it is actually short.) The goat's head changed
to that of a bull. The bull asked. (Traveler, what is
happiness?) I answered: (Your question and my
answer are happiness.) The bull's head became a
lion's head. The lion asked. (Traveler, what is
love?) I answered. (You are a lion; I am a man.
Love is you and I at this moment in time sharing

the same space.) Suddenly the lion changed into a lovely young Arab woman. She held a lamp in her hand as she walked. I followed her. We came to a tent. I followed her inside. Suddenly I had the body and passion of a young man. Time passed. The fierce winds of confusion died down; the rough waves of illusion settled. When eventually I came out of the tent, I had the lamp in my hand. I threw the lamp into the night sky. The lamp flew off into the night sky. The lamp became the moon (it changed to full moon, half moon, crescent moon.) Blue moonlight lit the desert. Time passed. Suddenly the earth's axis began to quiver. At a distance, a great shape rose out of the ground. A sphinx like creature, it had the head of a man and the body of a lion. A camel train appeared in front. Meanwhile the tent and the woman had disappeared. I looked at the crescent moon and thought of the woman. (Her touch, her breath, her soft glossy hair. Oh Artemis, oh the heartbreaking illusion of that night!)

24

I got back on the horse; we continued our journey.
I lifted my head and looked at the crescent moon.
In the distance I saw a grand mosque standing in
the moonlight. Minarets surrounded the golden
dome; four pillars split the sky. I embraced the
majesty of the scene, wonder in my eyes, praise in
my heart. We traveled on. Suddenly I heard a
voice within me. (Look, a place where your soul
can breathe; the eternal is beside that watering
hole.) I reached a hand toward the crescent moon.
I could not reach it. In the starlight reflected from
my hand, I felt the woman's touch. (Your eyes,
your dimples. O Diana, I feel your passionate
seductiveness, the coolness of your lips.) Once
again my heart crossed time and I stood in the
freshness of youth.

25

We reached an oasis. I got off the horse. A wooden bench stood at the water's side. I sat on the bench and looked abstractedly at the surface of the water. The moon shone faintly on the water in the billowing mist. The water was a dreamy valley, the world of the nymphs, with a magical fountain that spewed unfathomable depths of light into the sky: the light was the eyes of earth that will not sleep until the end of time, the eyes of Gaea, the lens of the eternal.

26

A dazzling luminescence flowered on the water.
The radiance of illusion spread through the water
like the ribs of a fan. Suddenly, a pair of dolls,
male and female, emerged in the light. Dressed in
splendid wedding array, they held hands
affectionately within the circle of light and danced
like ballet dancers. I was crying. Who was this
dancing couple? They danced happily on the stage
of light. I had a sad memory from the past. An
amorous couple emerged from the distant recesses
of consciousness. They truly loved each other.
They were not one but two, not complete but
incomplete. Ultimately they were flowers that had
failed to bud. The woman dreamed eagerly of a
love nest; the man longed for freedom. And so he
sent her away. She left his side smiling to the end
through flowing tears.

27

I was engrossed in the dancing pair. My tears flowed without end. What were my tears about? Regret, failure to achieve, yearning? The horse neighed and shook its head. Time to leave. I got up off the chair and mounted the horse. No words, just an emotional sharing that perhaps provided the gift of solace. The horse took a turn around the outside perimeter. Slowly it distanced us from the oasis. I didn't look back. I couldn't look back. The dolls were within me. They were in my heart. They blinked like starlight as they danced within me.

28

We turned into the ruins of an abandoned village.
Human remains were everywhere. The horse
walked very slowly. The dried up human remains
held me deep in thought. (Bones, bones) where
have your bodies gone? Your dreams, your blood,
your flesh, your spring season, your light, your
flowers, your loves, your songs, your memories?
Where has life gone? Your beautiful smile, your
fragrant breath, your blue soul, yesterday's
beating heart?

29

The horse stopped at the top of the village. An old crone with flowing white hair sat quietly on a bench. She had a lamp in her hand. She looked up at me. Her eyes emitted a blue-green phosphorescent light. Lamp in hand, she got up off the bench and approached me. She reached out the lamp to me. I took it but said nothing. She sat down on the bench again. The horse moved off and gradually pulled away from the village. I could feel her fierce gaze on my back. She was now a golden Buddha, a cross-legged sitting Buddha, a stone Buddha. The stone image turned back into the old crone. She kept looking at my back. In the dark, her eyes were sparks of a blazing fire.

30

How far had we gone? A great lake appeared
before my eyes. The water glittered like a
wondrous emerald. I got off the horse. To one
side there was a small folding chair; a fishing pole
dangled in front. I sat down; I put the lamp on the
ground and looked vacantly at the water. All my
life I had been a keen fisherman: (Scoop net; troll;
fish pot; weir; bamboo weir; keep net····)
I recalled a twilit autumn evening when I sat on
the river bank with a fishing pole dangling over
the water. I experienced a spiritual awakening, a
moment of foreknowledge; I heard an inner voice.
When you are over 70, fishing takes on a different
meaning. (You are not fishing time or fish; you
are not fishing philosophy, you are not fishing a
moment, you are not fishing the eternal. Fishing
means plucking something forgotten, something
lost, some innate natural truth from the waters of
the heart, from somewhere deep in your

consciousness. It is a will to return to origins, a yearning for the fetal; it is the subconscious at prayer.) Time passed. I took the pole in my hand. There was a nibble on the line, an unexpected nibble. I'd caught something big. I felt a heavy pull in the water. More than 30 cm, I thought. I yelled with delight, aware of a tingling frisson. A deep, sharp thrill gripped me. But I wasn't fishing for fish. I threw the pole into the water. At last the moment had come, the moment to forego everything, to stop the struggle, to give up fishing pole and fish and the long time I had devoted to these pursuits and to do so without regret. I was facing a new truth. For the first time in my life I knew the pain of the fish on the hook.

31

Lamp in hand, I got on the horse. We traveled for
a long time through the darkness. Suddenly the
horse stopped. From a distance I saw spirits—weird
demon shapes—approaching in a line. A dreary
blue light clouded their eyes. They came within a
few steps of me. I hurled the lamp at them.
Flames soared in the air. The flames wrapped the
spirits in an instant. Screams ripped the air.
The spirits disappeared in the red flames. The flames
quickly became a great ball of fire, which rose
violently in the air tracing a tangled path through
the night sky. Eventually it flew away and
vanished on the far side of darkness.

32

We were going through fields now. I don't remember when we got out of the desert. I lifted my head and looked at the night sky. Clusters of stars and a crescent moon dotted the sky. I saw a star falling. It traced a long tail of light as it fell on the other side of the sky. I watched its track as it disappeared into the dark. I was buried in thought. Pitiless, the life of man; ephemeral, the vestiges of earth. Boundless pathos; existence without a name; dim memories; scattered dreams, my life had vanished like a falling star.

33

The horse pulled up. I got off. A golden washbasin
sat on three legs at knee height. It was half full of
water. A second crescent moon floated in the
water. There was a clothes hanger shaped like a
tree beside the basin. A white cotton cloth hung
on it. I dipped my hands in the basin as if to
stroke the crescent moon. The moonlight slipped
around my fingers. I splashed water on my face
with my moonlit fingers. I stroked my beard.
A pristine energy hung like incense in the air.
I reached my hand to the clothes hanger, took the
cloth and wiped my face and hands.

34

I got on the horse. Time passed. We reached a great windmill. An old man sat there on a horse. Rusty armor covered his skinny body. The horse was old and worn, like a corpse; only a skeleton remained. With his long pole the old man kept tilting the windmill, and he kept muttering something indecipherable. The old man's body was emaciated but his sharp voice held a resolute dignity and a noble pathos; every gesture had sublime conviction and a sense of inviolability. Time passed. The horse moved on, leaving the windmill and the old man behind to fade into the distant plain.

35

We stopped in front of a high stack of straw. A few
mischievous boys romped around the stack. I smiled
contentedly as I watched them. Time passed.
A child emerged from the stack of straw and
approached me. He stretched his hand out shyly
and handed me a slingshot and a stone. I put them
in my pocket. The child slipped back into the stack
of straw.

36

The horse moved through distant, uncharted plains, bound always for the endless horizon. Such was the expanse of darkness through which we moved. But the motion of the land was different from that of the night sky; the sky, totally composed, had stopped all movement. Crescent moon and star clusters had ceased their motions. Two forms, locked in their unchanging places, looked down on the earth. Suddenly a carousel appeared. And I was a child on the carousel. I had the illusion of spinning in one place on the carousel. The horse moved resolutely forward, pushing away the earth as it advanced toward an invisible destination.

37

The horse stopped in front of a stream. A stone
hump-backed bridge lay over the stream. The horse
hesitated at the entrance to the bridge. A one-eyed
giant stood at the center of the bridge. Quickly I put
the stone in the slingshot, raised my hands and
aimed at the giant's forehead. I pulled the slingshot
tight and fired the stone. There was a great crash.
The giant tottered and fell headlong into the stream.
He did not move; he was apparently dead. The horse
snorted; reassured, it began to cross the bridge.
It stopped at the center of the bridge and stood
there in perfect inaction; it didn't even breathe.
Time passed. The water in the stream trickled by.
That tiny resonance awakened space and cosmos,
whispering the principles of unceasing creativity
and destruction. The horse quietly lifted its head
and shook its tail. Ears pricked, mouth quivering,
the horse moved on. A little faster now. It crossed
the stone bridge and then slowed its stride. The
giant had not moved.

38

The horse reached a primeval village, took a few
steps forward and stopped. (Full moon) the natives
were naked and they had gathered in the center of
the village. Dry tree branches lined the ground
and a naked corpse lay on them. A fat old woman
of short stature with a garland on her head led the
ritual for the dead. In her hand she had a long
stick twisted at one end like the antlers of a deer.

39

Eyes closed, stick lifted in the air, the old woman recited an incantation. (As if in response) the others closed their eyes, raised their arms and murmured u-u, shu-shu, p'u-p'u in imitation of the wind. Time passed. The old woman finished the incantation and opened her eyes. Hips swinging gently, eyes rolling, the old woman kept repeating something. A man approached the corpse. The old woman stopped all words and gestures. The man hunkered down at the head of the corpse. He said nothing, just looked in the eyes of the corpse. Living eyes and unliving eyes shared space and time, but they were looking at different worlds, floating in different seas. Then, muttering gently to himself, the man patted the shoulder of the corpse. He stopped speaking and kissed the corpse on the cheek. Then he struck a flint and lit the fire.

40

The old woman began murmuring again and the others circled the corpse and began to dance. The flames burned high and consumed the corpse. The body of the deceased soon disappeared in the sacred flames. The people danced with greater fervor (as if intoxicated by the twilight glow). Suddenly sadness filled my heart. Tears I couldn't control spurted from my eyes. Eventually the fire burned itself out and song and dance came to an end.

41

The man approached the cremated remains and took some bones from the ashes. He put the bones on a flat rock and crushed them to powder with a stout stone. He distributed the powdered remains of the deceased among the crowd. They rubbed the bone powder on their faces and applied it to arms, legs and bodies, as if giving themselves a dry wash. The old woman beat her stick on the ground as she repeated her prayer. The crowd danced in a circle. They sang as if they were happy. They continued to sing and dance, intoxicated by feelings of union and delight. I watched them with tear filled eyes. No one was aware of my presence. I was an outsider. I cried alone in my grief.

42

The horse moved on, gradually distancing us from the funeral. Tears continued to flow down my cheeks. I couldn't stop them. The more I tried, the more my feelings burst into tears. I was abstracted in thought. (What is truth? What is nature's law? What is rationality? What is irrationality? What does savage mean? What does civilized mean? What is ignorance? What makes sense? What is barbaric? What is enlightened? I was crying in the face of death, while they were singing. I was sad while they danced; I was melancholy while they celebrated a festival.)

43

The horse stopped in front of the gate of a tiled house. A yellow lamp hung under the eaves. I got down off the horse and knocked on the gate.
It slid gently open. I went inside. Mats were spread here and there in the big yard. People were sitting on them. They sat in twos and threes at simple drinks tables as they talked quietly among themselves. They were dressed variously. Some wore traditional clothes but one group wore turbans.

44

Although I was the focus of attention, I kept looking away. A short interval elapsed. A man approached. He was middle-aged. He wore a black bamboo hat and a white outer coat. He greeted me and directed me to a place to sit. I sat on my own on a mat. He turned away and disappeared on the other side. I bowed my head. Folks kept looking over at me. Eventually a young man dressed in a black suit brought over a small drinks table and set out a few side dishes.

45

I poured the wine from the gourd bottle and it slid
slowly down my throat. It was like drinking the
wine of the Immortals; the sweet wine tasted like
dew. I emptied cup after cup. Slowly the wine
mood came over me. Awareness grew hazy.
Feelings of happiness engulfed me in a flowering
haze. And when the bottle was almost empty,
feelings of sadness pushed back in. Folds of grief
wrapped me round; it was as if I were buried in
fog. I poured the last of the wine. I put down the
cup, got up and began to dance. The mourners
looked at me with surprise in their eyes. My
shoulders moved in the joyful ecstasy of the
dance. Then something wonderful happened.
The mourners got up in twos and threes and began
to dance. The drinks tables disappeared and the
yard became a splendid dance stage, a sumptuous
banquet. I saw a wondrous scene. Priests and
people swayed in the dance, performing a ritual to

console the dead on the journey to Nirvana. Their eyes were filled with delight and conviction, with anxiety and terror. An aura of emptiness mingled with sadness could not be hidden.

46

I came out the gate. The horse stood there like a stone horse on guard. I got on the horse and moved off. I looked at the lamp under the eaves. My tears began again. The yellow light of loss made me cry. I looked at the night sky. In the far reaches of the sky, one star shone with exceptional brightness. I felt the spirit of the deceased had cultivated a flower of remembrance, a poem of past time. The starlight was a symbol of transcendence. It represented a return to the origins of wind, cloud and the immortal.

47

The horse and I walked the earth, just the two of us, two become one. This was our final walk. We were unique creations under the sky. The horse stopped. I waited. A short interval intervened. The horse did not move. I heard the horse whinny.
It shook its head and whinnied gently, sadly. I sang a sad song in my heart. (Do not cry, friend. I know your sadness, your suffering, your inner pain. I know your God given nature, your mission to guide me from this world to the next, from the physical body to the spirit, from the red dust to paradise, from this moment to the eternal moment. Be not sad, my friend. Your voyage is not complete. You are God's messenger, the bringer of consolation, the companion of my soul, the ferryboat of mercy. I know, friend, your integrity, your honesty, your transcendence. I know your sadness in walking this last stage with me. My friend, it is for me, for me.)

48

The horse walked on. The horse walked the
surface of the earth and approached the edge of
darkness (stride, by stride, by stride) at a pace
suited to the search for truth. I saw for the first
time the land of death. I began to breathe it in.
Moon and stars smiled overhead; beneath the sky
I felt the night and the silence of creation.
The horse stroked the lungs of eternity as it walked
toward the land of the gods, the home of the soul.

49

Who am I? I reviewed my life calmly. All my life
I embraced change; I lived with commitment.
I dreamed of a better quality of life, a more
productive future for mankind, a more passionate
pulse. I always called out to the young. (Young
people, the time has come. Rise up, waken up,
begin, act. Young people, sharpen your blades.
Breathe passionately; let heat fill your souls.) And
I shouted again. (Young people, don't give your
lives to the word success. Let your objective be to
share the fruit of success. Young people, the sense
of emptiness that follows success, the willingness
to share the feelings of defeat—these feelings
spring from a lack of human love. Young people,
make common ground of your success with those
who have failed. Share the bounty of success with
those who lag behind. Young people, dream of
revolution, dream the ideal, dream of
powerlessness. Let passion lead you in effecting

change. Let freshness bloom the flower of hope in our world. Let the throbbing life-force sing our tomorrows.)

50

My life has turned to foam. I have attained nothing, neither change, revolution, hope, nor a sense of future. I leave nothing behind in this world. And yet I achieved. I achieved many things. I achieved everything. At this moment in time, here in this place where I no longer exist, in this world I have left behind, someone else is crying out to the young.

51

The horse stopped. We were at the end of the earth. I held my breath and looked at the dark sea. A bird flew up off the surface of the sea. In the distance I heard a seagull shriek. The sound stirred the pulse of my deepest being. A shuddering loneliness gripped me, coupled with feelings of wonder. I felt my soul reverberating deep within me. Suddenly anxiety and terror—difficult to bear—enfolded me. I was terrified, like a child. I wanted to run away, to go back. I wanted to turn the horse's head and race back crazily to the world of men.

52

Tears burst out, rolling down my cheeks. Idle tears flowed in the face of empty dreams and vain hopes. I knew it was impossible to turn around, to go back. But that didn't explain my sadness. We had reached the end of the earth, the borders of the world, the limits of thought. This was the first principle of my sadness. I couldn't bear it. I was in a vortex of emotion. I got off the horse and fell to my knees. Hands propping me on the ground, I wept like a child.

53

A hunchbacked dwarf wearing an old world
headscarf stood in front of me. He reached me a
handkerchief without saying anything. I took it
and wiped my tears. I turned my head to return
the handkerchief, but I couldn't see him; he had
disappeared. I pressed the handkerchief to my
eyes. Eventually, I got up, folded the handkerchief
carefully and put it in my pocket. I straightened
my clothes, walked over to the horse and stroked
its mane gently. The horse didn't move; it gave
itself to my touch.

54

I got on the horse and looked up at the night sky. A star from the lapis lazuli sky fell at great speed into the night sea. The star cut through the thick darkness and a mysterious shining arch rose from the spot in the sea where it fell. A thick sea fog surrounded the arch. The horse reached the sea and began to walk on the surface. It went toward the shining arch, crossing the water as if it were walking on dry land. The horse reached the arch and went right through. It followed the lengthy corridor of light for some time until eventually an exit appeared. The horse went through the exit. The sea fog and the arch disappeared, and a star shot up into the sky and lodged there. Darkness swallowed horse and man.

55

How far had we gone? The moon was covered with clouds and fog; the sea was calm. A glimmering diminutive figure floated toward me from a distance. A terrapin stood before me. It stood on its turtle flippers and looked up at me. Those glittering eyes. The turtle greeted me. (My Lord, I'm here to escort you. The dragon king has summoned you.) The horse followed the turtle into the sea. The turtle lit the depths and led the way like a pair of headlights. A little later we reached the dragon palace. The horse followed the turtle toward the dragon king's throne. Fish ministers stood there in rows: Minister Dolphin, Minister Hagfish, Minister Shark, Minister Marlin, Minister Octopus, Minister Sea Horse, Minister Mermaid, Minister Sting Ray, Minister Starfish, and many others from the depths of the sea whose names I didn't know. They all stood there gazing solemnly at the visitor.

56

The horse pulled up. The turtle made dutiful obeisance to the throne, once with hands joined, and once on bended knees. Lovely mermaids on each side of the throne fanned the king; one held a pheasant feather fan, the other a white feather fan. The turtle returned to its place quickly. Eventually Minister Octopus spoke. (Traveler, you must give us your heart. The dragon king needs your heart to treat his sickness. Traveler, do not think reproachful thoughts. Do not decline the opportunity to serve the best in the world. Show perfect altruism, demonstrate agape, effect benevolence. Your death will not be in vain.)

I knew now I had been deceived. I tried hard to disguise my fear. I looked up blankly at the Dragon King. Unlike the half fish, half human form of his ministers, the Dragon King was totally human. He held a crane fan in his left hand. His face, greatly emaciated, had a sickly pallor, but his body was quite the opposite, fat and wobbly.

57

I took the handkerchief from my pocket and quietly wiped my eyes. The Dragon King lifted his crane fan; his ministers held their breath in reverential fear. I looked around at the assembly with composure. I sighed a little and wiped my tears with the handkerchief. The Dragon King spoke. (Truth Seeker, what's wrong, why are you crying? (I'm sad,) I said, (because I left the golden heart at home.) The ministers were a little discomfited. Time passed. The Dragon King raised the crane fan. The assembly grew quiet. The Dragon King asked, (Truth seeker, what is the golden heart of which you speak?) (It is the cure for all disease,) I replied, (the key to immortality. It is a mysterious medicine that cures all disease; it is the medicine of resuscitation.) The Dragon King stared at me. (Do you mean to say you have no heart in your breast?) he asked. I put my hand on my breast. (Indeed, I have a

heart,) I said. (What does your heart do?)
The Dragon King asked. I said, (It is not what you
seek. It is just a piece of useless flesh. It cannot
cure disease; it serves no purpose.)

58

A discussion ensued. Many opinions were voiced.
Each speaker had his own fervent point of view.
The Dragon King listened quietly to the opinions
of his ministers. A considerable time passed. Finally
the Dragon King spoke. (Enough, enough, My
Lords.) They ceased speaking. (I will speak,) the
dragon king said. (In my opinion, Lord Starfish
and Lord Sea Horse are correct.) The Dragon King
looked at me for a moment. I bowed humbly. (Truth
seeker,) the Dragon King said, (you must go home
and bring back the golden heart.)

59

The horse was back on the surface; the moon had cast off cloud and fog and the turtle's eyes were lighting the way. The turtle said, (My Lord, you mustn't delay. The Dragon King's condition is very serious; every hour is vital. A minute is a lifetime; a second is a year. As soon as you get home, you must get the golden heart and bring it to the palace without delay.) A moment of silence ensued. I said, (Turtle, turtle, foolish turtle, the golden heart is in its wonted place in my breast; it is intact. The heart beats the same for the rich and powerful as for the lowly and ordinary. It is the wonder medicine that cures everything.) The horse moved away slowly. I heard the despairing cries of the turtle behind me. (Disaster, disaster, this is a disaster for the great one. So poignant, so sad. I groan, I moan, it's all been in vain, useless, all gone wrong. What's to be done, what's to be done, what's to be done for his majesty the king?)

60

An island appeared in the offing; it rose from the sea like a lamp, a giant sea creature on the surface of the water. The horse turned toward it. When we were almost there, a torch appeared in the distance. We reached the island and slowly approached the torch. The horse stopped in front of the torch. I felt my blood run cold. A weird bodily form stood in front of me holding the torch (the torch burned bright red.) The form was dressed in priest's black garb with a hood, but under the hood there was neither face nor anything else, just empty darkness.

61

Suddenly the torch form spoke. (Pilgrim, I was waiting for you. Follow me, please.) I followed the burning torch onto the island. I saw that while he was clearly holding the torch there was no sign of a hand. The flames of the torch fluttered in the sky. Strangely, I no longer had any sense of fear. It was as if I had entered a temple, as if I had stepped into a sacred place, I experienced an unbelievable sense of peace and tranquility.

62

We walked for some time. The torch form stopped.
I looked around. (Crescent moon) A dilapidated
pavilion stood in front (it had a straw roof turned
up at the ends.) A candle was burning on a bronze
stand at one end of the pavilion floor. A bowed
figure hunkered at the far side of the floor, like
Rodin's self-portrait. And an illimited solitude
flowed beyond the straw roof. The night wind
tickled the grasses, which were wet with dew.
A dim sadness enfolded me. I felt an unbearable
emptiness. My eyes brimmed with tears. I gazed
through my tears at the bowed figure.

63

The bowed figure got up and walked toward me through the grass, keeping the straw pavilion behind him. He was dressed in rags; long hair covered his shoulders. His eyes were pristine blue. He stopped two paces in front of me and looked into my eyes. The stark light in his eyes cut through me revealing my impenetrable soul. He and I looked at each other, our mutual gaze reflecting another me, a bronze replica, familiar, yet unfamiliar. Time passed. On the other side of the pavilion, two faceless forms dressed in white priestly garb stood side by side, carrying a huge cross. They kept appearing and disappearing. The figure in front of me turned to look at them.

He raised his eyes to heaven and walked toward them. He reached his back toward them. They put the cross on his back and then stepped to the side.

64

(With the cross on his back) he began to walk toward the sea. We followed in silence. We walked 12 paces. Increasingly, the burden of the cross was beyond him. Sweat dotted his forehead; his breathing grew harsh. The weight of the cross on his shoulders was excruciating. His upper body bowed till it almost touched the ground. His gait was reduced to a crawl. Finally the sea appeared. He walked another few steps and stopped. (Sweat ran down his spine) groans and heavy breathing proclaimed his inner torment. I put my hand in my pocket and took out the handkerchief. (I reached out a hand) to the torch form who came over to me. He took the handkerchief with his non-existent hand.

65

The torch form took the handkerchief to the
suffering figure. The handkerchief floated in the
air. The torch form followed, approaching the
suffering figure and wiping the beads of sweat
from his forehead with the handkerchief.
The handkerchief was wet with sweat. With great
difficulty the suffering figure turned to look at
me. He began to walk again. The others stood
there; no one followed. It seemed at any moment
as if he would fall. Step by step he dragged the
cross along the ground until he reached the sea.
He stopped all movement and took a labored
breath. The breeze blew from the bamboo forest.
The torch flickered in the clear breeze. Time
passed. The suffering figure looked up at the
night sky. Starlight flickered in the distant sky and
infiltrated his eyes, sparkling there with dappled
effect. I focused on the distant empty sky; I was
buried in a web of thought. The horse and I stood

there—sculpted rider on horseback. It was as if life's flow had stopped in a solid space. The torch no longer burned; it was frozen into a sculpted piece. I pushed my thoughts aside to look again at the suffering figure. He was moving again.

He trudged forward into the sea and buried himself in the ordeal of the dark, in the sea of suffering. I cried. Silently I cried. Tears flowed, silently they flowed. I looked at the sea. For the longest time, I stood there and looked at the dark. (I looked at the sea he had walked into, the sea that had called him, the sea that had swallowed him. Free of ideas, free of thought, no worries, no desires, no inner fixations, the sea of silence that had lain there since primeval times.)

66

In the meantime the torch form handed me back the handkerchief. I took it. The sweat, breath, and stench of bitter loneliness of the figure who had returned to the sea permeated the handkerchief. I folded it and put it in my pocket. The torch form kept the sea at his back and began to walk into the dark. The torch grew further and further away until in the end it was lost in the dark. The horse moved off. It went quietly toward the sea. We reached the sea and stopped for a moment. The horse was buried in thought. It walked on again, on the surface of the water. The sea was quiet, cruelly peaceful. The sea was fast asleep, endlessly replete, buried in a distant dream.

67

The horse was walking slowly toward some distant place. Step by step⋯ the horse's hooves jangled on the surface of the water; its kick movement produced an indifferent, monotonous sound.
The sky was above us; the sea was beneath us. Silence throughout the earth. The horse and I, existence and space⋯ the pathos of the fourth dimension spread everywhere, uncaringly. Suddenly a sigh escaped from within me. Grief pushed out like a stormy wave. My eyes filled with tears. I heard a voice. I heard moaning from deep sea deposits on the bed of darkness, a monologue of pain, and the anguish of struggle.

68

Finally we reached land. The horse strode through the plain. There wasn't a tree in sight. I heard a cat meow. The sound rolled around the ear and then dispersed in the empty sky. The dry grass crunched under the horse's hooves. The wind was loaded with the smell of the earth; it felt prickly on the face. Suddenly I was tight-chested, unable to breathe. Nausea rose in my throat. After a little while I saw corpses scattered along the ground. There were drops of candle grease here and there, and pools of water from bodies rotting in the mud. Naked bodies, some still breathing, bones hideously bared, moaned in distress.

69

The horse pulled up. I dismounted and approached
the bodies. I looked into the eyes of each in turn.
They did not move. They did not recognize me.
It was if they were stuck to the ground. There was
no reaction, they stared at the sky with empty
eyes. My tears flowed again. I cried like a fool;
I couldn't stop. I saw their living grief, the pain of
non-death. I felt they craved death not life, dissolution
not eternal life. Death would be a mercy, a blessing,
a joy beyond measure, an infinite grace.

70

Suddenly I had a thought. I crossed to the other
side and squatted on the ground. I scraped the
ground like an animal and made a little hole. I put
my hand in my pocket and drew out the handkerchief.
I put it gently in the hole. Then I buried it carefully
in the clay. A little later an apple tree sprang up.
I got up and stepped back several paces. The tree
spread its branches; soon it was a mature tree.
I stood back another few paces. Clusters of apples
clung to the branches. Then the apples began to
plop to the ground. Soon the fruit was heaped
under the tree. The plopping sound reverberated.
It was enough to waken souls. The dying began to
crawl toward the tree. Foam clotted their lips as
they reached out grimly. Finally they got to the
apple tree. They wolfed down the fallen apples.
Immediately their strength returned. There was
fervor in their breath and a blue sparkle in their
eyes; their faces shone and chubby flesh returned
to their bodies.

71

The horse pushed through the plain without resting. I looked up at the night sky. In the distance the crescent moon and the star clusters guarded their places as they had from the beginning; same places, same unchanging smiles; same illumination of the earth. And in the midst of that beauty I saw another concealed shadow. It was an object of pity. Night descended, and when the darkness awakened, destiny revealed its light for the first time. A sad history that faded with the morning sun.

72

The shadow was me, my name, my history, my destiny. In this night, in this darkness, where this song ends, I will fade with the dawning of the day, a speck of dust, an illusion. Myth tells us where our destinies meet. Was that the explanation? The stars smile a plaintive smile as they look down on me. And I cry tears of sadness when I look up at them. (In my eyes) they see their tears reflected in silence. In a moment of communion, their smiles and their tears bloom a great garden of flowers.

73

I looked all around. The horse had reached an ancient abandoned city. It was a vacuum space without human trace or warmth, where even the breath of silence had disappeared. A sense of solitude pressed on the heart; the atmosphere was oppressive. The horse trotted to the center of the ruin as if crossing through time. The clear clip-clop of the horse's hooves shook the dead earth and poured into the plumage of the sleeping gods.
(A little later) the horse reached the end of the city.

74

The horse pulled up. A group of old men sat a few paces in front. They wore traditional overcoats. Their white hair was so long it reached the ground. They sat on tree stumps at a circular table. A small lamp adorned the center of the table. They were talking to each other in low tones. I couldn't hear what they were saying. It was like pantomime, I couldn't hear a thing. Whisper, whisper, I wondered what they were saying. Folktale, legend, allegory, ancient tale, strange anecdote, tale of a hero? Were they talking philosophy, literature or religion? I was very curious. I just wanted to understand. I wanted to go closer and listen to the conversation. The horse stood there without moving. I wanted to get off the horse and approach the group, but I couldn't move. I had the heart to move but not the physical power.

75

The old men argued stubbornly in a struggle of minds and bodies. Finally they got up and became as one body grouped around the lamp. Hands held high in the air, they looked up at the sky. Suddenly a whirlwind spiraled from the ground; like a great pillar it soared into the sky. When the whirlwind ceased, the old men touched heads, and as if comrades all their lives, they muttered in a language that was indecipherable. The sound grew violent. Time passed. The sound gradually lessened. (Suddenly) the round table, the tree stumps, the lamp and the old men solidified like a rock. The rock then became an armful of a shade tree. Round table, old men, and tree stumps disappeared. Only the lamp remained on the top of the tree. Like a bird's nest, like a lighthouse lamp, it sat on the uppermost branches of the tree and gave off a mysterious light.

76

I looked at the lamp. The light gently massaged
my eyes. The warmth infused my retina; the heat
flowed into my heart. How can I describe the
feeling? It was a sensation of warmth and
abundance, of gentleness and fragrance, like my
mother's breast when I was a child. It was a
moment of heartwarming liberality, a gesture of
patience, gratitude and peace. I was wrapped in
pure beauty and overflowing abundance. I fell
into reverie as if in a dream. A spell of enchantment
took me to distant memories, sucked me among
ancient bookcases. I was lost in a vague
homesickness. I dusted the layers of dust from the
pages, let the ink of enchantment fly and brought
the dead letters back to life. My mother's faint
smile in an old sepia portrait came back to life. I
took her smile to my heart and wept for joy.

77

Time passed. There was a thunderous boom and the shade tree began to shake. Suddenly the tree became a lighthouse. Then the boom stopped and the shaking subsided. I saw the lamp become a lantern on a tower. The lighthouse illuminated the night. The horse moved on. The lighthouse light followed us and shone on my back. We left the lighthouse behind. With heavy stride the horse went slowly through the plain of darkness.
The searchlight followed the horse leaving a long finger of light in our wake. Time passed. Eventually the finger of light stopped and the lighthouse stood in its tracks. The horse did not stop. I didn't look back. We passed beyond the circle of light and disappeared into the desolate land of death.

78

I saw a group of mummies. We skimmed past. Heads consistently down, they walked like robots toward some undefined point. One of them stared at me. A cold beam of light came from sockets that had no eyeballs. I felt a shiver run down my spine, followed by goosebumps. With sprightly gait the horse distanced us from them.

79

We traveled on for a bit. I heard a quiet melody in
the distance. The horse went toward the sound.
I listened closely. The melody got nearer and nearer.
We came to the source of the music. The horse
pulled up. A round marble table stood on the ground.
A music box waterfall sat on top of the table. I got
down to the ground. I looked at the music box.
A carousel turned within a glass ball.

80

The carousel kept turning on its axis within the small glass ball. I saw that the small glass ball was the world of men. And the small carousel was the lives of men. Suddenly I had a vision of permanence. A feeling of cold emptiness swept over my heart. Human life was a moment within the unending kalpas. I had a new awareness of the gulf of sensibility. A current shocked my inner being. Evanescence, evanescence, the evanescence of existence···· An unexplained despair wrapped my soul.

81

Time passed. Man and horse moved through the maze of space and time. Withered brush rolled along the ground. A pigeon fluttered its wings and flew into the air. An eagle circling in the sky dive-bombed and snatched the pigeon. More time passed. A few grand old trees still stood among dead trees with bared roots. The horse stopped in front of an aged chestnut. An old man dressed in tatters, hair all gone, was knocking chestnuts with a long bamboo pole. (I remember throwing stones to knock chestnuts when I was a boy.) The chestnuts fell out from burst burrs. At times the burrs fell straight to the ground. The ground was covered with chestnuts and chestnut burrs. Suddenly chestnuts and burrs changed into books. Shell and bone, stone, clay, metal, bamboo, wood, papyrus, parchment, paper···· An array of ancient texts··· philosophy, religion, literature, theology, art, medicine, history, astronomy, geography, law, biology, rhetoric, geometry, astrology. The old man stopped knocking the chestnuts. He leaned his bamboo pole against the tree. And when he did so, the books changed back again into chestnuts and burrs. The old man burst the burrs with his feet. He took out the chestnuts with his fingers. Some burrs had single nuts, some had twin nuts. He threw them on the ground. When finally he saw a burr with three nuts, he took out the nuts carefully and held them in his hand.

82

The old man turned toward me. He reached me the three chestnuts. I took them and looked at them in wonder. They sparkled like jewels in my hand. The old man went back to the chestnut tree and leaned against the trunk. He drew his legs together, bowed his head and wrapped his arms around his knees. I looked in that direction. There was no one there. The old man, the chestnut tree, the nuts, and the burrs were all gone. There was no sign of the bamboo pole. The horse moved off. I was buried in thought. Who was the old man? Where had he gone? Why had he given me the chestnuts? I searched for answers. There were none. I put the nuts in my pocket. We went about nine paces. A name suddenly came into my head. Diogenes, the beggar philosopher from ancient Greece. Was the old man Diogenes? Was Diogenes the old man? I had no way of knowing. I just remembered his name. And his name lit up like a lamp inside me.

83

I felt the flux of time; I heard the tears of space.
I heard the song of sad souls wandering the earth,
the grief filled melodies of insubstantial things,
deep and blue. The horse and I were headed to the
end of night. (In the past) morning always waited
at night's end. Hope in the morning sustained me
through the black night.

84

I searched anxiously through memory. I heaved a
great sigh. Regret swept through me. In that distant
place, man's place, the cyclic world waited for
morning to come again at the end of night.
Without doubt the new morning would open its
eyes again. Ah but I could no longer call morning
forth. I could not embrace the morning. At the same
time, I couldn't forget morning either. Nor could
I wipe it from my consciousness. I was heading
straight for the end of night, but morning did not
recognize me. I could no longer look on morning.
I could not hope to embrace morning. From the
fringes of long night, where light, darkness and
dissolution intersect, I was being drawn blindly
into the disintegration of morning.

85

The horse reached the bank of a river. There was a brushwood bridge. We crossed the bridge and continued a little further. A hut emerged.

The horse stopped in front of the hut. A young boy lifted the straw mat that served as the hut's door. The boy was naked, 6 or 7 years old; he had a fleshy body and his head was shaved.

86

The boy came over to me. His eyes sparkled as he reached out his hand. I put my hand in my pocket and took out a chestnut. The boy took the chestnut with a smile. With the chestnut in his hand he went into the hut. I got off the horse, lifted the mat door and followed him inside. I stood there without moving for quite some time. The boy was nowhere to be seen. I called him in my heart (Boy, boy, boy····) Where had he gone? Where was he hiding? Where was this place? In time-space terms where were we? Nothing met the eye, neither space nor object. Deep, black primeval darkness blocked my sight.

87

My breathing was the only sound that echoed through the darkness. Time passed. The darkness did not lighten; in fact, it grew gradually thicker. Suddenly a light shone in my eyes. Automatically I closed my eyes. A little later I opened my eyes again. Something glimmered hazily in my sight. Eventually I saw a young man sitting in front of me. He had a notebook open on a miniature desk. A tiny smart phone was set beside it. The young man sat on the ground. His eyes were on the flashing screen as he tapped the keyboard. The sound spattered aridly in all directions. (How can I explain this?) I felt a sense of emptiness that threatened to implode my heart. I was weighed down by oppressiveness. I thought I might choke at any moment. It was unbearable. I ran out of the hut. I was out of breath as if I had run a long way. (Cold sweat trickled down my back.) My body was bent double; I was gasping for air.

88

The horse lifted its head in fright. Its great round
eyes looked at me directly. Was it in sympathy?
It was (the first time for the horse) to look intently
at me like this. I straightened my back and took a
deep breath. My breathing slowly returned to normal.
My eyes filled with tears. The horse was still looking
intently at me. We stood there for a while looking
at each other. Night was withdrawing; the stillness
of the plain was palpable. The melancholy of space
and the sadness of the atmosphere were in the
dripping of the night dew. Each blade of grass
reflected bitter longing; the world was immersed
in the loneliness of distant seas. Moon and stars
looked down silently on us.

89

I got on the horse. The horse stood there without moving. I felt a gentle shiver, a movement of agitation. The horse was shaking. Burdened by thoughts of the bitter mission with which it had been entrusted, the horse neighed gently. I waited. I lifted my head and looked at the distant sky. Tiny teardrops ran down my cheeks.

90

I examined the air around me. A dim pulse that was neither life nor death enfolded me. Weak breathing and plaintive feelings reduced me to tears. I knew the end was coming, the end of a long journey. The moment of dissolution into eternity was beckoning. Tears fell, tears that were both hot and cold. There was no fear or regret or sadness. What can I say? I felt a faint sense of longing that defies explanation, a vague yearning, a desire that resists definition, colors unseen, echoes unheard, a sense of loss that chilled the bone.

91

The horse moved off. Time passed. We moved beyond the flow of space into the mysteries of time, a concept of time that was long and ancient. The horse pulled up. A meerkat stood in front of us. I took a chestnut out of my pocket and threw it a few feet in front. The meerkat raced over and cracked the nut with its teeth. The meerkat ate the chestnut and changed to a monkey. The monkey changed to Neanderthal man. Neanderthal man changed to homo sapiens. This last mentioned turned his eyes on me and looked intently. Two shining eyes gleamed coldly. Anxiety, knowledge and melancholy were coiled in those blue depths. And as we looked intently into each other's eyes, there was a sharing of feeling without words. A strong current flowed from heart to heart, a free flowing sense of history, a Zen movement to the origin of thought. He and I, two essences united in thought, affected a return to unity of being. Homo sapiens turned away and disappeared into the dark.

I saw the night sky. The air lightened. The crescent moon became a glorious full moon. Dew sparkled on the grass; insects buzzed on the ground. I opened my ears quietly and focused on the splendid banquet. Time passed. Suddenly I recalled an episode from my youth. I was a lonely, sensitive boy. Pistachio twilight colors dyed the gathering evening light. I slipped out of the house. An irresistible force pulled me to the hill behind the house. I sat on the grass. I was alone, completely free, without dog or companion. A blue light tinged the darkening air. Buzzing grass insects broke the stillness. I looked down on the village nearby. Clusters of simple thatched farmhouses were scattered through the landscape. The smoke of evening fires spiraled from chimneys on sharply pitched roofs. (Suddenly) an unexplained sadness swept in on me. I longed for someone whose name I didn't know. Cold penetrated my heart. I was gripped by an emptiness that was hard to bear. Drops of dew fell. I sat there on my own, crying dispirited tears. I was filled with sadness. Suddenly the blue light disappeared and black night swallowed everything. I got up. I fell into a moment of oblivion. I didn't know who I was, or where I was, or what I was supposed to do. In the end I came down the hill and turned toward the house. I followed the dark, winding lane to the front of the house. I pushed the brushwood gate; the bells rang. The kitchen door opened and mother ran out and folded me in her arms. I felt a sudden surge of sadness. I began to cry again. Tears flowed down my face. The tears wet my mother's bosom. Moon and stars looked down on the reed fence. I heard the cuckoo cry on the hill. I closed my eyes. And I prayed. (That this is not a dream, this moment, mother and I. Let me hold this dream in my heart for a long time⋯) in her soft breast, without distinguishing joy from sorrow.

93

The horse strode into the shrubbery. Blue tinted
moonlight lit the tops of the citrus. A parched
musty wind blew among the branches. I could
hear the whispered breath of the shivering leaves.
There was something bleak and ominous in their
shallow breathing, signs of wounds that didn't
appear to the eye. We continued on for some time
and eventually came out of the shrubbery. In the
distance there was a farmhouse. I approached.
The house was old and leaned to one side; it was
dreary and derelict like a shriveled snail.

94

The horse went into the front yard; there was neither brushwood gate nor hedge. A few steps in front there was a single door with a tiny built-in window. There was no light in evidence or sign of human presence. Suddenly the wind whipped up the dust on the ground. The wind gradually strengthened and soon the yard was a scene of chaos. I closed my eyes tightly. The horse stood in the wind like a bronze statue. Time passed. I sat on the horse with my eyes still closed. I had no idea how long we were there; perhaps the notion of time itself had disappeared.

95

Anxiety gripped me. I was swept up in a fearsome wave of terror. (I felt as if I would disintegrate in the air.) My terror was a tree that had neither roots nor trunk. If I jumped off the horse and got my feet on firm ground, I felt my terror would dissolve. Terror dug deeper inside me. Just when I thought I could no longer control my fear, the gate creaked. The wind abruptly hid the sound. I looked at the gate. It was slightly open but it wasn't moving. Time passed. The gate opened and two people came out. They stood in front of the gate and looked directly at me. They were weird, grotesque figures and they stank so badly I wanted to puke. They were an aged, diminutive, skeleton couple (retaining human form with difficulty). They had white hair like a bird's nest and were wrapped in a veil that covered them to the ground.

96

I looked at them with fear and disgust. Time
passed. The old woman approached. She reached
out her hand. Her hollow cheeks and ghostly eyes
clearly spoke of a great inner longing. I put my
hand in my pocket, took out a chestnut and gave it
to her. She trembled violently when she got the
chestnut. Shudder or spasm, it was hard to say,
but it was certainly a stormy wave of passion.
Cries continuously escaped her shrunken lips.
She approached the old man. They cracked the
shell and divided the chestnut evenly between
them. Something mysterious happened. Husband
and wife changed into a young couple. The yard
immediately brightened. It was an eye-dazzling
phenomenon, the light of life, the spark of youth:
the couple generated the light of a beautiful
gemstone.

97

The couple opened the door and went into the house. A kerosene lamp flickered inside. I could hear the night wind blowing through the bamboo grove at the back of the house. The lamplight soon weakened. There was a gentle rustling sound in the house. In the distance the scops-owl screeched. Time passed. Inside the house a baby's first cry rang on the air. This was soon followed by whimpering baby cries. Hushaby baby, the young mother sang a lullaby, which quickly ended the baby's cries. Time passed. The door opened. Three people came out into the yard. I saw the young couple and a cute boy child standing there. The horse moved off a few paces. I turned my head and looked at the three. They were still standing there. They turned toward me with happy faces and waved.

98

Time passed, how much I can't be sure. We were on a narrow country path, going through paddy fields, along a river bank, following the curves of a hill. The horse crunched through the snow. Big fluffy snowflakes were falling; there was neither moon nor stars in the sky. The wind was down.

I recalled winter nights from long ago when I lay down by the brazier and listened to my granny's stories. The stories were frightening and mysterious, sad and interesting. The big flakes fluttered down; the paper in the doors rattled. I never managed to hear the stories to the end. Granny's voice and the whispers of the night acted like a lullaby from an old fable. (Tonight I must listen to the end) come what may. Inexorably I sank into the land of dreams.

99

The full moon showed again. The snow had stopped. The night was lightening. Brilliant moonlight illumined the snowy fields. (The horse dropped its head) while I rode straight-backed through the snowy fields, evoking the image of a centaur--half horse, half man. Horse and I, the two of us, man and horse, companions in a common project of enlightenment, were traveling together through the world after death. Soulmates, we were a metaphysical grafting of two trees, two yet one, one yet two.

100

The horse left its first and last hoof prints on the virgin snow. We walked through the margins of time as if on a cloud. Powder snow was falling. I looked intently at the distant edge of the dark. Beyond the hazy horizon, a memory came back to life. A snowy winter night. For several hours mother and I had been walking the snow road. No matter how far we walked the end of the road got no nearer. All that appeared to the eye was the night and the dark and a huge cotton wool eiderdown that covered the world. Between snowflakes, I heard branches snapping under the weight of snow. I held on to mother's hand; I was walking resolutely with short quick steps. Mother had a parcel under her arm; with her other hand she held my hand. The walk was tense and driven.

101

I was bursting to pee; I dribbled before I told mother and she let me pee. I have a fun memory of the moment. I was hunkered in the snow. With my finger I wrote the words (Mother, I love you) in the snow. She kept calling me, telling me to hurry up. She had a lot on her mind, but I didn't know what was bothering her. (War, calamity, confusion, ideology, thought, conflict, confrontation, greed····) I didn't know what they meant. Mother grabbed my hand and pulled me after her, walking with grave urgency. I kept looking behind. Big snowflakes were falling on the words I had written, but the words did not disappear; if anything they became more distinct. This is another childhood memory that is indelible in my mind, engraved like a star in the depths of memory.

102

The horse moved through the snow as if in a dream. I was vaguely aware of its breath. Breath, wind, monologue, anxiety, moan, pulse, lament, bitter grief, echo. Ultimately it was the echo of self, of a soul weeping tearless tears, a wordless lament, a soundless cry, the cry of a soul heading for that distant primal place, the home of the spirits, the world of God and the eternal. The cry was my pitiful resistance, a tiny frantic act of defiance, a last ditch upheaval; it was pent up anger, deep, hollow resignation, a weakening pulse, a cry from me and my life--one final gesture on earth, a grand desire to adapt, a cry of self-renunciation.

103

The time for parting was getting near, departure from life to death, from death to a new life, from the end to a beginning, a moment of terror and tremulous excitement. My head was buried in the margins of consciousness. I was not aware of self. I stood there for a moment, lost to self, looking at the airy world around me. Beads of dew formed in my eyes; cold tears flooded my cheeks.

104

The horse pulled up at the entrance of a very old church. I got off the horse and climbed a narrow flight of stone steps. There was a holy water font in front of the door. I dipped my fingers in the holy water, made the sign of the cross and straightened my clothes. I opened the door quietly and went inside. It was a broad dim space with all the solemnity of a church building. A little to the front, a candle burned quietly on a long wooden candleholder. There was no sign of a lectern or of a cross. A purple curtain hung behind the candle. I meditated for a moment, looked at the candle and approached. I stopped a few steps in front. I genuflected with reverence; hands joined I bowed my head and closed my eyes. And I began to pray silently. (Merciful One, take pity on my soul. Look graciously on me. Benevolent One, receive my soul. Welcome me. O Holy One, take me to yourself.)

105

I got on the horse. Time passed. An imposing
residence appeared in front. I went towards it.
The horse pulled up. My eyes drifted to the upper
window. A vague sadness crowded in on me.
My heart was heavy; a groan escaped my lips.
More time passed. The light flickered; the curtain
lifted; the window opened. A young woman
appeared. She leaned on the window frame and
looked at the night sky. She examined the full
moon with shining eyes. She brought to mind
poetry, the moon, Sang'a—the moon nymph, a
window, my soul, Aphrodite. I looked at her.
Tears flowed. I called her fondly; I called her
wistfully. She didn't hear me; she didn't know
me. My voice failed to reach her. Her eyes did not
respond. If I reached out a hand, I could touch
her; if she stretched out a hand, she could take
mine. But the experience was a fiction, an
illusion, a heartrending fancy, a mournful

phantom. Existence and space, the gap between time and memory, an invisible wall, eternity stood between us.

106

I could feel the sea; its breath flowed in the wind. The horse continued on slowly through the trees. The wind in the trees echoed desolately in my ears, the leaves trembled. Time passed. We came to a remote temple. A hanging lantern burned gently in the silence of the night, lighting up the front of the dharma hall. The horse approached the lantern and circled it as it would a pagoda. Wind bells tinkled in the dawn breeze. They whispered in my ear. (Seeker of truth, seeker of truth, look for enlightenment. Go back to things as they are.) The horse came out of the temple and moved on beyond the palace of annihilation. Tak-tak-tak-tak the wooden clappers echoed from the dharma hall. The horse continued on, passing the timber windbreak. We reached the edge of the cliff. My mouth was dry; I was aware of a strange thirst. The horse pulled up. I saw a huge crock jar a few paces off. I dismounted and approached the jar. It was brim full of wine. As I was about to scoop the wine with my hand, a storm petrel fluttered over. It had a thread in its beak.

When I opened my palm, the storm petrel dropped the thread and whooshed off. I lifted the thread. It changed into a gourd on a string. I scooped wine in the gourd and drank. (So sweet) a foretaste of immortality perhaps? Or the nectar of eternal life? I slaked my parched throat and the thirst disappeared. A feeling of serene self-satisfaction, a sense of pure vitality flushed the depths of my senses. I floated the gourd in the wine barrel and got up on the horse. Suddenly a well-house appeared on the wine barrel. The wine barrel changed into a circular covered well. The gourd became a bucket on a rope. The horse moved on. Step by step, as if performing a solemn ritual, it approached the edge of the cliff. The horse brushed against the well. A frog croaked in alarm. We went a few paces. The frog stopped croaking. A willow tree sprang up beside the well. The extended willow branches covered the top of the well. The willow branches danced gently in the breeze. I was vaguely aware of a sad sound within me. (I heard a willow break in tonight's song;

who would not be filled with thoughts of home?)
Cold waves broke against the foot of the cliff.
(Then) I heard the foam gently whispering.
(Living being, do you know that death is neither
beginning nor end? Death is the dissolution of the
cells, a change in form from seen to unseen.
Living being, compose yourself. There is neither
joy nor sorrow nor regret. Remember, truth is
immutable; truth, and only truth, is one. Existence
has left the cycle of life and death. That is destiny.
All things are ephemeral. The ephemeral is all
that remains.)

107

The horse pulled up. The edge of the cliff was seven paces away. The clear breeze washed my ears coldly. I lifted my head and looked at the night sky. The full moon suddenly became a crescent moon. A myriad stars were embroidered in the sky as if scattered by silver dust. In the glimmering starlight I was searching for something I could not identify. What was it? Memory, a cellular need, an irresistible instinct, a struggle for return, my inner life; a manifestation of the unconscious sleeping deep within it?

I was aware of a human presence. I saw a woman standing on the edge of the cliff. (Chignon, black skirt, white blouse) she was looking at me in silence. I got off the horse. As soon as my foot touched the ground I became a child. The woman opened her arms. I ran toward her and snuggled in her arms. She hugged me gently. The child closed his eyes; tears flowed down his cheeks. An unidentifiable joy surged through his heart. A dizzy abundance wrapped his body. Her hand ruffled his hair. He was enveloped in a sense of peace. He dreamed a sweet dream, happy as a fetus in the womb. She kissed his forehead. He heard her whisper in his ear. (Baby, baby, my baby, you have finally come. I've waited so long. My lovely baby⋯⋯)

108

I was a baby again, a baby on the breast. I was in her arms. I could hear her heart beating. She held me upright. She rubbed her cheek on mine.

Her breath was gentle and so fragrant it made me giddy. I burst into giggles. She turned and looked at the sea. I heard the sea breathing, asleep in the moonlight. A black-tailed gull lighted on her shoulder. Suddenly the bird was gone; white wings had sprouted on mother's shoulders. With a smile on her face she looked into the eyes of her baby. She flapped her wings and flew into the sky. Wings flapping gently, she flew to the edge of the sky where she melted among the stars.

Two became one, a star, a star, a star that emitted a twinkling light. The horse stood alone on the ground, a protecting agent, it remained there like a wooden horse. The horse did not neigh.

No, that's not right; the horse neighed, tearfully, tearfully, in lament. (And yet) it wasn't neighing,

it wasn't neighing. There was no sound. Cold
inaction, awful emptiness. All tears, all sorrow
sank into the silence at the bottom of the deep
blue sea. The horse was buried in thought, eyes
closed, buried in self-effacement. A considerable
time passed. The horse did not move. The horse
was neither dead nor alive, neither existent nor
non-existent, neither visible nor invisible.
The horse was a thought, consciousness,
transcendence, an ideal, sadness. It was poetry,
loneliness, delay. What was in the horse's mind?
Suddenly I heard a distant sound. The horse and
I both heard the sound. The song of God and man,
of life and death, of heaven and earth, of sea, wind
and waves, of meditation, of cliff and rock face,
of foam, moon and stars, of night and eternity.

🎴 Lee Chondo's other works

Love Song of the East (2016) :
a long dramatic poem.

Man loves in the name of imagination
and imagines in the name of love.

Record of the Defeated (2017) :
a collection of short stories.

Loneliness is not that there is no one beside me,
but that no one lives inside me.

Children of the Cosmic Tree (2017) :
a long lyric poem.
(Myths and Legends of Jeju Island)

When our minds are filled with fog,
human nature is confined within.

The Truth Seeker

© Lee Chondo 2014

Translation © Kevin O'Rourke 2017

Miraesung Publishing Company
62, Sangdo-ro, Dongjak-gu, Seoul, Korea
All rights reserved
Tel. (+82)2-3280-2096 / Fax. (+82)2-3280-2096
Mail: Miraesung7@hanmail.net / duutaa@naver.com

First published in English edition 2017

ISBN 979-11-958899-3-8